The
Nicest
Naughtiest
Fairy

Nick Ward

The Nicest Naughtiest Fairy

First published in 2006

by Meadowside Children's Books

185 Fleet Street, London, EC4A 2HS

Text and illustrations © Nick Ward 2006

The right of Nick Ward to be identified as the
author and illustrator of this work has been
asserted by him in accordance with the Copyright,
Designs and Patents Act, 1988

A CIP catalogue record for this book
is available from the British Library

Printed in Indonesia

ISBN 10 pbk 1-84539-149-7
ISBN 13 pbk 978-1-84539-149-2

ISBN 10 hbk 1-84539-150-0
ISBN 13 hbk 978-1-84539-150-8

10 9 8 7 6 5 4 3 2 1

The
Nicest
Naughtiest
Fairy

written and
illustrated by

Nick Ward

"Oh good!" thought the naughtiest ever fairy,

as a fat little envelope popped through her letterbox. "Perhaps someone has sent me a present."

But it wasn't a present. It was a letter from all of her neighbours, and this is what it said...

Dear Naughty Fairy,

STOP being so naughty! We've had enough of being turned into toads and trolls and wobbly jellies. If you don't stop your naughty tricks we will drum you out of town!

Lots of love from your friends,

Giant, Big Bad Wolf, the Butcher, the Baker, the Boiled Sweet Maker, the Three Little Pigs and the Lord Mayor

"**Oops,**" thought the naughtiest ever fairy. She didn't fancy being drummed out of town, so she decided to be a well-behaved little fairy.

Starting straight away!

The very noisy giant was busy
crashing about, spring-cleaning
his castle when the well-behaved
naughty fairy arrived.

"I can help you with that,"
she shouted above the din.

GRANNY GIANT.

"**No!**" cried the noisy giant.
"I know your naughty tricks."
"Don't worry, I'm a well-behaved naughty
fairy." She smiled sweetly
and waved her
magic wand.

But although
the naughty
fairy tried to be
good, her magic
was determined to
be especially naughty,
and almost at once things
started to go wrong...

KAZAM!

Paintbrushes whizzed through the air, sloshing paint over the walls, the windows and the giant as well!

The vacuum sucked up the rubbish,
the rugs and just about everything else!

Soon it was so full,
it exploded in a cloud of dust.

"**Sorry,**"
said the good naughty fairy
and quickly flew off to help
somebody else.

The Big Bad Wolf was trying to huff and puff a house down.

"Oh, please let me help," volunteered the good naughty fairy, and summoned up a wind so strong it blew the wolf's clothes right off and sent the house spinning across the valley and far out to sea...

"**HELP!**"
shouted the three little pigs
who were still in the house.

"**Don't worry,
I'm coming,**"
cried the naughty fairy.

But on the way,
she met someone else
who needed her help...

The boiled
sweet maker
lived at the top of
a steep hill and he was
mixing a huge pot of sweet
smelling candy, when the
naughty fairy passed by.

"Don't interrupt me now," puffed the candy man. "I have to finish all the sweets for the Mayor's very important procession."

"Oh, let me help," cried the well-behaved naughty fairy.

And before the sweet maker could shout 'No!' she had waved her magic wand.

KAZAM!

WOOSH!

The pot began to rattle and shake, and WOOSH! the gooey mixture erupted out of the pot, spilling across the floor. "Stop it!" cried the sweet maker as the sticky mess bubbled out of the door and down the hill. But the well-behaved naughty fairy had already gone.

All the way down the hill townsfolk were getting stuck in the mucky mess. The Mayor's important procession had been bought to a standstill, up to their knees in toffee.

"I might have known it was you," yelled the Mayor, shaking his fist as the naughty fairy flew by.

Soon the naughty fairy came upon the bold and roaring lion
(who was king of the jungle). He was having a royal nap.
"Ah, he's sleeping like a baby, said the helpful fairy.
"I'll just make him a little more comfortable."
She waved her magic wand and...

KAZAM!

The mighty king of the jungle awoke to find himself dressed in a baby's bonnet and nappy, rocking in a cradle!

"How embarrassing," he roared.

"Just you wait!"

Big Bab

But by now the naughty fairy had flown out
to sea to help the three little pigs,
whose house was still bobbing
about on the waves.
"Fairy to the rescue!"
she cried, waving her
magic wand...

KAZAM!

A huge and
hungry whale
arched out of the
sea and gobbled up the
pigs and their house
in one mouthful!

Up through
the clouds
it swam,
turning and
somersaulting
and emitting
polite little burps.

(A house is a substantial
meal after all, even for
an enormous whale!)

"Come back,"
called the good naughty fairy,
waving her magic wand...

KASPLASH!

The whale belly-flopped into the village pond.

("Oof," gasped the whale as the little pig's house shot out of his mouth).

Yipee!

FLOP

Pond water and pond life rained down on the town. Mrs Munchet, the schoolteacher, was covered in slime and weeds and frogspawn...

KASPLOSH!

The baker's magnificent cake for the Mayor's procession was drenched in pond water...

And the last of the fiery dragon's fiery breath was snuffed out in the downpour.

"This is one of the naughty fairy's tricks," they spluttered.

"**Oh no!**" cried the well-behaved naughty fairy, desperately waving her magic wand as it rained frogs and newts.

But **POP!**

Her naughty magic turned one of the frogs
into her naughty new friend, who was
delighted to see the mess the naughtiest
ever fairy had made.

POP!

All the townspeople
marched up to the well-behaved naughty fairy.

What a state! They were covered in slime and toffee and duckweed.

(The naughty fairy couldn't help but giggle).

"Are you responsible for this shambles?" demanded the Mayor.

"It's not my fault," complained the well-behaved naughty fairy. "I've been good, but my magic was naughty."

"Tidy this mess up," ordered Mrs Munchet.

"And no magic, or I'll turn you into a sausage!" added the naughty new friend.

Ignoring the naughty new friend, the well-behaved naughty fairy waved her magic wand to start the big tidy up, but...

KAPOW!

"That's not fair," grumbled the naughtiest ever sausage, as she started the long task of mopping up.

"In future I'm going
to stay naughty...

It's safer!"

For Jade,
Who thought I had forgotten her!

N.W.